Born In Time

Born In Time

The Christmas Story

By Mildred Cram

Illustrations and Cover Design by Louann Jordan

the sunstone press

Santa Fe, New Mexico / 1972

First Edition

Printed by Starline, Albuquerque, New Mexico
Printed in the United States of America
ISBN 0-913270-10-5

Born In Time

The Christmas Story

The Welcome Inn stood a little back from Highway 101 between Buellton and Los Alamos in California. Painted barn-red with white trim, it was as neat and bright as any motel on the coast. There was a wading pool for children in front, a small garden in back. All around it there were fields where cattle grazed. Whenever traffic on the highway eased up for a moment, the silence was absolute. But then fleets of trucks would come ploughing past and flocks of silvery buses and whole schools of desperate speeding cars, and the noise would begin again. For this reason, Mr. and Mrs. Watson, who owned the place, had built with great care. The Welcome Inn was almost sound proof.

During the Christmas holidays they placed a small tree in each of the ten units. The ruby and blue lights cast a sort of stained glass pattern on the walls and ceilings. And so faint as to be almost inaudible, hymns and carols were piped over the audio system, soothing the taut nerves of the tired motorists so that they forgot the hazards of the road and slept like children, relaxed and safe.

Christmas meant a great deal to the Watsons. Every card they received . . . and there were many, sent by guests who remembered them with affection . . . they put on display in the "office." They didn't care for the humorous cards, declaring that Christmas honoured One they dearly loved . . . it wasn't meant to be a rowdy holiday. They taped

"For the tenth time Mr. Watson got up from his chair, opened the door and glanced out."

plastic snowflakes on the window-panes and tacked up boughs of fragrant evergreens and sprigs of holly, then sprinkled powdered camphor on the branches of the little trees.

Christmas eve, last year, Mrs. Watson sat in the "office" knitting with that air of abstraction so becoming to women of her age. The piped music coming from behind the grill on the wall hummed softly. All through December, hymns and carols had elbowed Dixieland jazz off the airways. Once more Bing Crosby dreamed of a white Christmas. Arthur Fiedler's sleigh jingled past again with sharp cracks of the whip. And Rudolph guided Santa's reindeer across the Arctic wastes, the forests, the frozen lakes, the sleeping cities . . .

For the tenth time Mr. Watson got up from his chair, opened the door and glanced out. The wading pool reflected a great blaze of stars, like a mirror held to the universe, and down on the highway at the foot of the drive a neon sign advertised the *Welcome Inn*. The word *Vacancy*, written in brilliant green, was visible a mile away.

A feeling of sadness weighed upon Mr. Watson's heart. As always on Christmas eve he thought of Luke's words: *And she brought forth her first born son, and wrapped him in swaddling clothes and laid him in a manger, because there was no room for them in the Inn.* It had always puzzled Mr. Watson how any inn-keeper worthy of the name could have been so unfeeling, so blind to the need of a gentle, expectant mother. Why hadn't the host offered his own room to the exhausted Mary and the anxious Joseph? Instead, he had snatched up a lantern and explaining that the Inn was crowded, had led the way across the courtyard to the stable. "You are welcome to sleep here. As you see, there's plenty of straw. And thanks to the animals it is warm enough. I won't leave the lantern since there's danger of fire. But the stars are very bright tonight."

A stable! Mr. Watson shuddered at the thought of it. Of course the great artists of the past had glorified the place, giving it form and grace, filling the broken roof with glimpses of angels and cherubims, a flash of wings, a swirl of draperies. It couldn't have been like that, of course . . . there would have been a trough where the animals drank, but no drain for the spilled water. There would have been sleepy chickens in the loft, and perhaps a family of owls on the rafters. The little donkey that had carried Mary on the long, difficult journey would have dozed nearby, twirling his great ears. A cow. A pair of sheep with moonstone eyes. Perhaps a big farm horse. And a cat, curled in a barrel, suckling her kittens.

Mr. Watson imagined that Joseph would have kicked forward some dry straw, loosening and scattering it to make a bed for Mary, who sank down with a deep sigh and a grateful smile for her husband.

Mr. Watson pictured Joseph as beardless, with a shock of white hair and black eyes. When he took off his coat to cover Mary, his only protection against the bitter cold was a woolen shirt, big-sleeved, open at the throat, banded at the wrists. A strong man, this Joseph, who stood with his fingers hooked in a wide leather belt, his head held high as if he challenged the world. As indeed he did.

It was more difficult to imagine Mary. Mr. Watson was a shy, courteous man and even in thought he hesitated to look closely at that lovely face. Her brow, her eyes . . . these the artists had painted. But could they have captured her radiance? That inner light? Could they have known that she moved in an aura that shone all about her yet cast no shadow? So that the straw bed where she rested was softly illumined and there was no need for the inn-keeper's lantern or the light of the stars . . .

"Close the door, Henry," Mrs. Watson said. "It does no good to watch. They're not coming tonight."

Mr. Watson glanced at the clock. "They might," he said. "There's still time."

"Only ten minutes, dear. At midnight we'll turn off the *Vacancy* sign and go to bed as usual."

"I suppose we're being foolish," Mr. Watson said. "There's not one chance in a million. Not one in a million!"

"Maybe next year," Mrs. Watson said with a comforting smile. "Now come in and close the door. It's very cold tonight."

But Mr. Watson remained on the threshold. Every year for five years, even when the *Welcome Inn* was booked solid for the holidays, Mr. and Mrs. Watson had reserved one unit on Christmas eve. It was set aside for some young couple who might be in desperate need of shelter. A wife already in the throes of childbirth, and a husband frantic with anxiety, and the nearest hospital twenty-five miles away. Surely, some such couple would notice the *Vacancy* sign and discover to their joy and relief that there was indeed room for them at the *Welcome Inn*!

Five times the Watsons had made the unit ready . . . the bedspreads turned down, the wall heater glowing, a supply of food in the kitchenette . . . plenty of milk and a big pan in which to boil water . . . Five years, and no one in need of their hospitality had turned up. Tonight, although a number of motorists had stopped and had offered to pay double the usual price for the unit, none of them met the requirements and were turned away with polite regrets and Merry Christmas wishes, but turned away nevertheless.

11

"I think I'll take a walk," Mr. Watson announced suddenly.

"Don't go too far, dear. You look a little tired tonight."

Traffic on Highway 101 had thinned to a trickle. To the north at the top of the grade the tail lights of a van pulsed on and off, then vanished over the crest. It was very cold and Mr. Watson turned up the collar of his coat. He went down the drive and walked south aginst traffic. The highway, its black surface shining with oil, stretched away toward the far, dim lights of Buellton. The fields were so dry, so trodden by the questing cattle that they looked as white as snow in the starlight.

As he trudged along the shoulder, Mr. Watson thought again of that night in Bethlehem. He wondered whether the guests at the Inn had been in a festive mood, drinking, carousing and singing ribald songs, while the serving maids ran for more and more food to heap the plates, and the wine kegs gurgled crimson streams into the flagons. And was Joseph angered by this, ready to rush across the courtyard and to strike frightened silence into the merrymakers with a great shout of furious protest? No. Mary would have held him back, saying that she didn't mind . . . there must be no quarreling on this night . . . "Come, Joseph. Let me have your hand. Stay beside me. I no longer hear the noise over there in the Inn. I hear instead a brushing of wings. Joseph, have you ever listened to the wild dove in flight? That loveliest of sounds, like the whistle of a fan? Stick upon stick, feathers upon feathers? That is what I hear now . . . and very far, very faint, a chorus of children's voices, clear as sweet water over white stones! Hold my hand, Joseph, and stay by me . . . The time has come."

Mr. Watson saw that an enormous truck was boring toward him, so he stepped closer to the wire fence and waited until it had passed. The roar and bubble of the great tires left him deafened for a moment; he put his fingers in his ears and shook his head. Then, quite close, he heard the custardy *moo* of a cow. He wondered why it was that cattle . . . and horses, too . . . so often leave their lonely pastures to stand near the high road. Was it possible that they craved human companionship? He spoke in a friendly way to the small Hereford on the other side of the fence and went on.

But the *moo* sound persisted, carried over from reality into the scene he had been imagining. It was such a strange sensation that it made him feel dizzy, almost as if the pull of gravity no longer attached him to the earth. To regain his balance he glanced up at the sky. He recalled having read somewhere that at the time of the Nativity Saturn and Jupiter were so close together that they appeared to be one.

Tonight, of course, there was no such display over California. And that was as it should be: in all the long history of man, only once had it been required of the two great planets that they slip out of their places and roll down the sky until their brilliance came together. Joined thus, disc upon disc, they drew the Wise Men out of the East and halted at last over Bethlehem, where, extending their long shafts of crackling light, they indicated to the weary travellers that here the new born King lay in a manger and that here they must leave their gifts of gold, frankincense and myrrh . . .

Mr. Watson had regained his balance. Nevertheless, he stumbled, and looking away from the sky saw that he was no longer walking along the shoulder of Highway 101 but was, rather, following a roughly paved street. He had entered an unfamiliar town. The street pitched steeply down between a

". . . the whitewashed walls were stained by what must have been centuries of rain and sun."

huddle of houses, almost windowless, flat-topped and square. There were no lights to be seen anywhere, but from a few chimneys smoke rose in blue columns straight up into the chill and motionless air.

Could this be an abandoned motion picture set? And, if so, why hadn't Mr. Watson known of it? But no. The cobbles beneath his feet were time-worn and real. The smoke had a pungent, unfamiliar smell . . . Olive? Cypress? The doorways of the houses were deep and strong, and the whitewashed walls were stained by what must have been centuries of rain and sun. A dog barked . . . or was it a jackal prowling the alleys of the town?

Mr. Watson felt a sudden chill of fear. As he hesitated, wondering what to do next, he heard the soft *moo* of the cow again. For some reason there was a link between this familiar, natural sound and the beginning of an experience beyond his understanding.

Deciding to waste no time in futile speculation, he hurried along the street hoping to meet someone who could direct him. Apparently everyone in the town was asleep, and Mr. Watson was reluctant to waken them by pounding on doors or shouting at the top of his lungs.

Then, turning a corner, he saw a glow of light below and heard a confused babble of voices. At the foot of the street there were several fair-sized buildings surrounding a paved court yard. A low wall encircled the place and Mr. Watson saw that a man was sitting there. Mr. Watson went up to him.

"I beg your pardon, sir," he said. "I have lost my way. Could you tell me how to get back to Highway 101?"

The man seemed to be deep in thought. He gathered himself out of his preoccupation with an effort and glanced up at Mr. Watson, smiling. Even sitting down, he looked extraordinarily tall. And yet there was a sort of hump on his back, a thickness between the shoulders. What caused this deformity was hidden beneath the voluminous folds of the long white robe he wore. His face was young, smooth, very handsome, the features aquiline, the eyes dark and luminous. Mr. Watson noticed that his feet were bare, strangely clean considering the dusty street.

"I live near Buellton," Mr. Watson explained, speaking very slowly and distinctly as Americans do when addressing a foreigner who might not understand English. "My name is Watson." He held out his hand. "Fred Watson. Proprietor and owner of the *Welcome Inn*. How do you do, sir?"

The young man took Mr. Watson's hand and shook it firmly with great friendliness and warmth.

"I am very glad to meet you," he said. With a gesture, he invited Mr. Watson to sit beside him on the wall. "May I ask — how did you happen to come here tonight?"

"The truth is," Mr. Watson said, "I don't know."

He sat down, feeling suddenly faint and unsteady. In spite of the cold, beads of perspiration stood on his face. He took out his folded handkerchief and pressed it against his cheeks, his forehead.

"I left the Motel only a few minutes ago," he stammered. "As a matter of fact, at exactly ten minutes to twelve." He glanced at his wrist. "But my watch says seven past seven . . . I can't understand . . ."

"A simple matter of geography and time," the young man interrupted. "Much too complicated to explain. Ignore the differences. You are in Now."

"Now?" Mr. Watson repeated. "It was Christmas eve

when I started out to take a little walk along the highway! December the twenty-fourth, nineteen seventy-two!"

The young man nodded. His eyes flashed in the starlight and he drew a quick, shallow breath. But he said nothing.

"This *is* Christmas eve, isn't it?" Mr. Watson insisted, with a note of desperation in his voice. And when the young man still failed to answer, with a sort of longing to make himself understood, Mr. Watson cried: "I know it is, because every Christmas eve my wife and I reserve a unit for very special guests: a young couple in great need of shelter. A child about to be born and a husband frantic with worry, and the nearest town many miles away. Tonight, as usual, we made everything ready in case . . ."

He broke off, glancing up at the stranger's face for reassurance, and, seeing there only polite attention, went on to explain as best he could.

"My wife and I," he said, "are probably very childlike. We look forward to Christmas as the most wonderful time of the year. Some people say it's gone commercial. That the old spirit is lost and that nowadays all it stands for is 'how many cards will I get and how many must I send?' Or: 'What did the Joneses give me last year, and how much did it cost?' But I've never listened to that sort of talk. I don't believe it. My wife doesn't believe it. That's why we plan this . . . this small kindness every Christmas eve. Dedicated, you understand, to Mary and Joseph . . ."

Mr. Watson broke off. "You know about what happened to them, of course? How there was no room at the Inn?"

The young man nodded. The babble of voices in the building across the courtyard diminished for a moment, then began again. And there was a sound of drunken singing.

"You have no idea," Mr. Watson went on, "how often my wife and I have wished that we might have lived when Mary and Joseph did. And that they might have come to *our* Inn! You may be sure *we* wouldn't have turned them away! The story of that Christmas eve has always hurt our hearts. The stable. The manger. So unfitting a place for the birth of our Lord! Please, sir, don't think me irreverent. But our Motel is very different from that. There are wall-to-wall carpets and heaters and wide beds with mattresses as soft as clouds. Lamps. Little kitchenettes with two-burner electric plates. Plenty of glass and china. Music. Or television if you prefer. A telephone . . ."

Mr. Watson lifted his head. "I am one innkeeper," he said proudly, "who would have made room for Mary and Joseph that night!"

He broke off again. His heart was pounding against the casement of his ribs and he trembled as if confronted by some mortal danger. *Where was he, really? Who was this calm and smiling giant of a youth?*

"I have already introduced myself," he began, "but I don't know your name. I take it you live here . . ."

"I come from very far away," the other said. "I haven't any name."

Mr. Watson hesitated before asking the question that formed suddenly in his mind. It must be phrased carefully, since the answer might solve the mystery of this strange experience . . .

"I'm rather tired and cold," he said finally. "Do you know of an Inn where I might spend the night?"

The young man turned his head slightly and pointed with a long, tapered forefinger.

"Yes," he said. "Across the courtyard. But I'm afraid there's no room tonight . . ."

"I know," Mr. Watson interrupted. "I know."

There was a brief pause. Then meeting the stranger's eyes squarely and summoning his courage, he asked: "And the stable? Show me, please, sir. The stable!"

"The building with the three arches where you see the radiance."

"Of course," Mr. Watson whispered. "The radiance. If you were to hold your cold hands close to it, they wouldn't be warmed. But if you opened your heart to it, if you exposed your soul to its rays, you would feel the heat of faith and would never be cold again . . ."

He got to his feet and stood for a moment, looking down at the miraculous light.

"This is Bethlehem," he said finally. "And Mary and Joseph are here!"

He turned with sudden urgency to the stranger. "I must speak to them," he cried. "I must offer them shelter. Quickly, before it's too late . . . unless, of course, the child is born!"

"Not yet."

"Then if we hurry . . . My own Inn is less than a mile away. If you will help me . . . Mary can ride and Joseph will lead the little donkey carefully, carefully. We can be there in a few short minutes. Surely, there can be no harm in *asking* them . . . "

The young man shook his head. He seemed to unfold, until he towered more than seven feet tall. The hump on his back suddenly divided and Mr. Watson, with a gasp of amazement, realized that he was winged. A few silvery feathers drifted to the ground and the points of the great, strong pinions scratched the cobbles as he turned.

19

"No," he said sternly, "you must not do this thing."

Then, as if he regretted his vehemence, he apologized: "Of course I know that you mean well. You want only to prove your love and your sympathy. But the Babe must be born here, and in a manger. There must be no change in the story. It must be told over and over again, down through the centuries, exactly as it happened!"

The young man put his hand briefly on Mr. Watson's shoulder.

"Oh, my friend, you are a good man or you would not care. The fact that you have cared so deeply all through your life only proves what I am saying: that if it were possible to change the story of the Nativity, what would its meaning be? And its value?"

The sound of laughter and singing grew faint again, seemed to recede . . . a retreating rattle of tambourines, a stamp of feet . . . back, back, until lost. And another sound beginning: woodwind, flute, recorder . . . a sort of breathless, sighing music . . . very far and faint . . .

"No. The story must happen as it was meant to happen. Think of the children who have learned it by heart," the young man said. "Think of the philosophers and teachers who have sought out its truth, and the priests who have explained it, each as best he can. Think of the mothers who have recalled it at the moment of delivery, taking strength from Mary's strength, and have smiled to themselves for having shared her joy . . . Think of these things, sir, and then ask yourself if you would deprive mankind of so precious a part of their spiritual heritage? The journey, the crowded Inn. The stable, the manger. The golden straw. The animals. All, all meant to be, and to pass from mind to mind, from heart to heart, as long as there is life on earth!"

"The young man put his hand briefly on Mr. Watson's shoulder."

The young man shook Mr. Watson's hand again. "I must go, now. I was chosen to inform some shepherds of the birth of our Lord and to guide them here, that they may see for themselves . . . The time has come." He added, as he turned away: "I don't believe you'll have any trouble finding your way back. Goodbye!"

As suddenly as if a shutter closed, it was dark where Mr. Watson stood. He could see nothing, not even the stars. He touched his shoulder where the young man's hand had rested and a thought shot through his heart like an arrow: *He was an angel* . . . !

Then the shutter . . . whatever it was . . . opened again, and there, blazing and glittering and shaking in the black bowl of the sky, were the stars. The Big Dipper. The Milky Way. Little stars. Big stars. All in their places. All part of the Great Plan . . .

And there, too, were the dry, white fields and the distant mountains . . . the highway and the fence. Mr. Watson heard the custardy moo of the friendly cow again. In the distance, he saw the tail-lights of a car just topping the grade, and the green sign: *"Welcome Inn Vacancy"* pulsing its friendly invitation. He caught his breath in a quick laugh, and in spite of his years began to run. He wanted to tell his wife what had happened to him: "I went to Bethlehem! I spoke to an angel! And do you know, I think he was the angel of the Lord?"

At that moment another car, coming fast from the south, passed him, braked with a screech of tires and turned suddenly into the Motel drive, its lights swinging across the units, then shining on the "office" door. It opened and Mrs. Watson stood there, silhouetted against the colorful glow of the tree, her knitting in her hand.

". . . Mrs. Watson stood there, silhouetted against the colorful glow of the tree . . ."

As Mr. Watson hurried up the drive, he saw a man jump out of the car, speak urgently to Mrs. Watson, then turn to help a woman who moved heavily, awkwardly, and who leaned against the man, her head against his shoulder. *"Could this be . . . ?"*

Yes. It was. As Mr. Watson reached the porch he saw that the new arrivals were young . . . both of them blond and slender, pale, with anxious eyes.

"When I saw that *Vacancy* sign," the husband was saying to Mrs. Watson, "I let out a yell! We were on our way to my folks in Santa Maria. I thought we could make it. But ten minutes ago, I knew we couldn't. My wife's starting to have her baby . . ."

"I know," Mrs. Watson interrupted. "Don't waste time explaining. Come with me. I'll show you your room."

She nodded toward Mr. Watson. "This is my husband. He'll bring your suitcases in and park the car. But first he'll call our own doctor."

She put her knitting aside and snatched down a bunch of keys from a hook above the desk. She was flushed with a dream-come-true look in her eyes. "We must put you to bed," she said. "Follow me. This way. Careful, now. And don't be frightened. You're going to be all right."

"Oh, thank you," the young wife whispered, smiling for the first time. "You're so kind. I'll try not to be a bother!"

Mrs. Watson wondered how she could explain that here at last was a chance to help compensate for the inhospitality of an inn-keeper who had lived very long ago. She unlocked the door of the reserved unit and opened it upon a warm brightness. The little tree with its ruby and blue lights glowed in the window. A chorus was singing "Silent night, holy night" to an accompaniment played by woodwinds, flutes, recorders . . . And Mrs. Watson, hesitating on the threshold, felt the satisfaction of the hostess who has seen to every detail and knows that her guests will lack for nothing to make them feel at home.

"How pretty it is!" the young wife said. "Are you sure you want us to stay? We have so little money. We can't really afford a place like this."

"Come in. Come in. There'll be no charge. This is our gift to you. From Mr. and Mrs. Watson of the *Welcome Inn*, with much love and a Merry Christmas.

In the meantime, Mr. Watson had hurried into the "office" to telephone the doctor. As he dialed the number, he glanced at the clock, then at his wrist. Both said that it was one minute to twelve. How had his watch managed to catch up with so many thousands of miles and years? Only a few minutes ago, in Bethlehem, it had been five hours slow . . . or was it fast? He would gather up his remembrance of everything that had happened, he told himself, as soon as he had attended to the urgent business at hand.

"I'll come right away," the doctor said. "And Watson? Don't boil any water! That's an old wives' tale! Just keep her calm until I get there . . ."

Then he, too, must have looked at the time, because he said:

"Merry Christmas!"

And hung up.

At that instant, over and above the singing of "Silent Night" bells began to ring. Piped into every unit of the Motel, they came from New York, Paris, London, Rome, wherever there were churches around the Christian world, all clanging and pealing . . . little bells, big bells, carillons, chimes, some

25

with deep voices, some with high, some that thudded, some that tinkled, some that shouted a great and joyous shout of welcome and triumph.

Mr. Watson felt his hair rise on his scalp; his finger-tips tingled. As he went to get the suitcases and to park the young couple's car, he saw that some of the tourists had come out in their bathrobes and slippers looking anxious and curious.

"Anything wrong, Mr. Watson?"

"No. No. Everything's fine A baby's about to be born. But the doctor's on his way . . . You just go back to bed, and in the morning I'll tell you all about it."

What was it he intended to tell them? Something wonderful that had happened to him. Well, he couldn't quite remember . . . Something about Bethlehem and a tall angel with great, strong wings . . . Something . . . Well. It was gone. No matter . . .

As he turned with the suitcases, the young husband took them out of his hands. "I'll carry these, Mr. Watson," he said. And then rather awkwardly he said that on the way up the coast he had thought a lot about how there had been no room for Mary and Joseph the night Christ was born.

"It sort of struck home . . . We hadn't expected the baby so soon, but just after we left Santa Barbara I knew we'd never make it to Santa Maria. It was too late to turn back. And all the motels were full. No room anywhere. Then we saw your sign! It was a kind of miracle, Mr. Watson. You two fine people taking us in . . . Yes, sir. A kind of miracle. I guess the story of the Nativity got through to you, too . . . !"

"It did indeed," Mr. Watson said. He went into the "office", switched off the *Vacancy* sign, then stood in the starlight on the porch, waiting for the doctor.

FINIS

Sell your books at sellbackyourBook.com!

Go to sellbackyourBook.com and get an instant price quote. We even pay the shipping - see what your old books are worth today!

000575S692

5692 000575

MILDRED CRAM was born in Washington, D.C., educated at Barnard and abroad. She began to write and publish in 1916. Since 1923 Miss Cram has lived in California. Her short stories have been published in **Ladies' Home Journal, McCall's, Cosmopolitan, The Saturday Evening Post,** and others. Her novels include the best sellers, **Forever** and **Kingdom of Innocents.**

In addition to her many novels and short stories, she is known for her work in motion pictures, radio and television scripts. Love Affair, Wings Over Honolulu, and Stars Over Broadway are some of the notable motion pictures that have had the special "Mildred Cram Magic."

Now, once again that "magic" is brought into focus on the traditional Christmas theme.